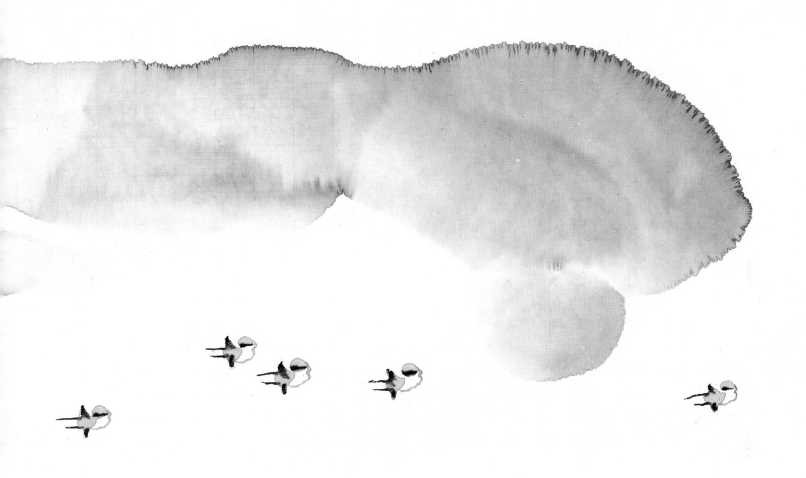

I Have a Zoo

Copyright © 2019 Shanghai Press and Publishing Development Co., Ltd.
Chinese edition © 2010 Guangdong New Century Publishing House Co., Ltd.

This book is edited and designed by the Editorial Committee of *Cultural China* series.

Story by Xiao Mao
Illustration by Liang Peilong
Translation by Yijin Wert
Design by Wang Wei

Copy Editor: Susan Luu Xiang
Editor: Wu Yuezhou
Editorial Director: Zhang Yicong
Senior Consultants: Sun Yong, Wu Ying, Yang Xinci
Managing Director and Publisher: Wang Youbu

ISBN: 978-1-60220-457-7

Address any comments about *I Have a Zoo: A Story of Animals All Around Me, Told in English and Chinese* to:

Better Link Press
99 Park Ave
New York, NY 10016
USA

or

Shanghai Press and Publishing Development Co, Ltd.
F 7 Donghu Road, Shanghai, China (200031)
Email: comments_betterlinkpress@hotmail.com

Printed in China by Shenzhen Donnelley Printing Co., Ltd.

1   3   5   7   9   10   8   6   4   2

The images on page 42 are offered by Quanjing and Getty Images.

I Have a Zoo

我有一个动物园

A Story of Animals All Around Me, Told in English and Chinese

By Xiao Mao & Liang Peilong
Translated by Yijin Wert

Better Link Press

I have a zoo with no walls or entry fees. It's open to everyone.

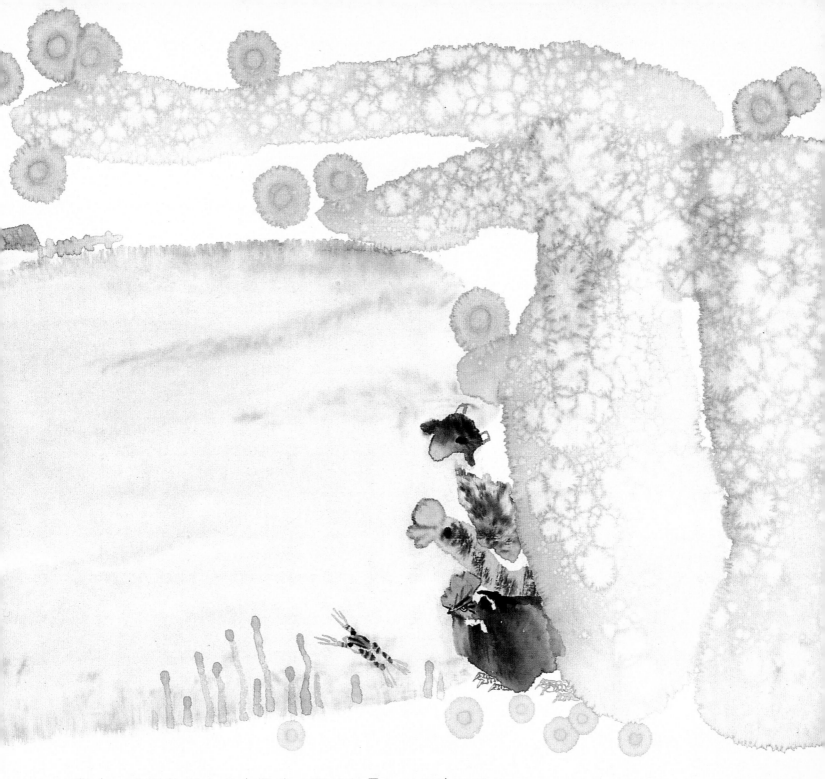

我有一个动物园，没有围墙，不收门票，对所有人开放。

Come on, everybody! Let's go!
小伙伴们快来一起玩。

The aquarium has small rivers, creeks, and ponds.
"Quack! Quack! Quack!"
Here come the grey ducks with flat beaks and the singing geese with the long neck.

水族馆有小河、小溪和池塘。
"嘎嘎嘎——"
灰毛扁嘴是鸭子，曲项向天是大鹅！

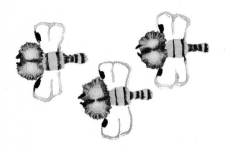

"Hey you, Goose! Don't run.
It's no good to leave the flock."

哎呀呀！大鹅大鹅你别跑，掉出队伍可不好。

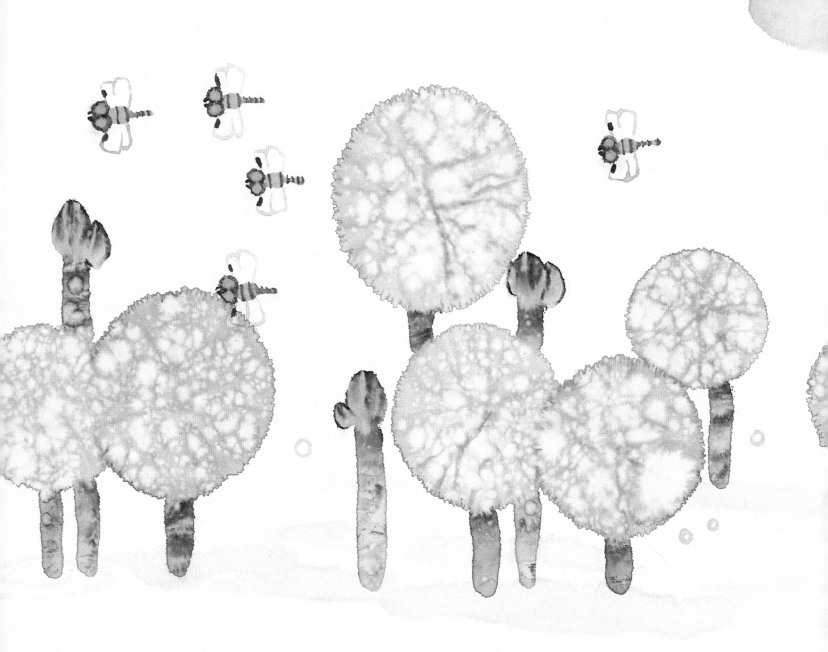

In the pond, the lotus leaf is like an airport.
The dragonflies are like airplanes gliding up and down the runway.

池塘里，荷叶飞机场绿油油。蜻蜓"飞机"飞上又飞下。

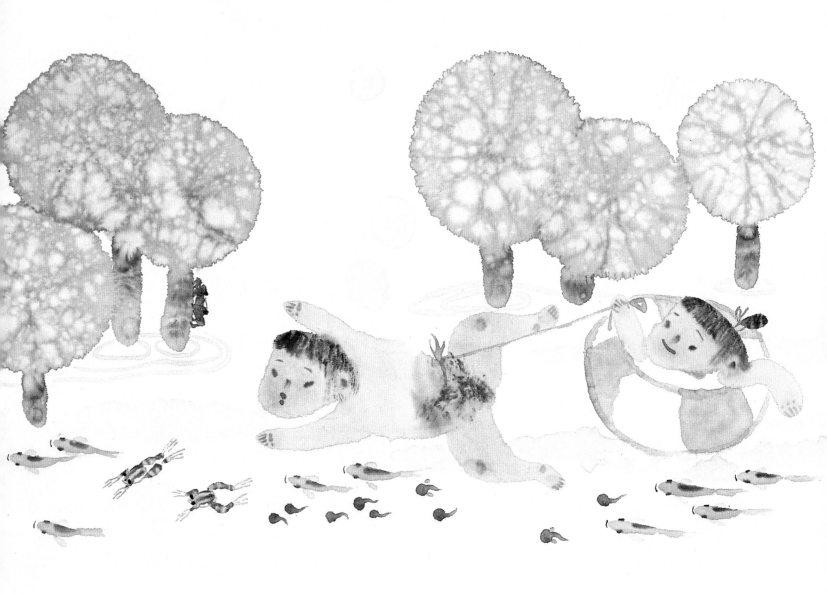

Streams are flowing and fish are swimming.
Eight-legged crabs hold their big pincers crawling sideways.

溪水流啊流，小鱼游啊游。
螃蟹八只脚，举着大螯横着走。

"Ribbit! Ribbit! Ribbit!" Frogs are singing together and slippery tadpoles are swimming.

蝌蚪滑溜溜，青蛙游啊游，"呱呱呱——"，一起大合唱。

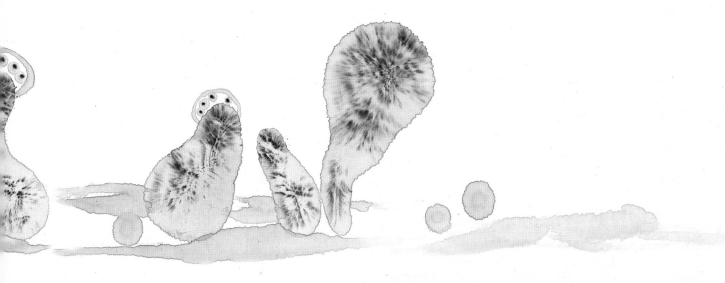

"Meh! Meh! Meh!"
The sheep drink water in groups and won't get lost.

"咩咩咩——"小羊去喝水，成群结队不怕丢。

"Meh! Meh! Meh!"
The sheep love to eat grass, jumping and running together.

"咩咩咩——"小羊爱吃草，蹦蹦跳跳一起跑。

"Woof! Woof! Woof!" The dogs are patrolling our zoo.

"汪汪汪——"，小狗来巡逻。

"Moo! Moo! Moo!" The big oxen are eating grass too.

"哞哞哞——"，大牛来吃草。

"Tweet! Tweet! Tweet!" They are the swallows.
Don't worry. We will visit them while they are nesting under the roofs.

"啾啾啾啾———"是燕子！住在屋檐不用怕，我们把他们来看望。

"Tweet! Tweet! Tweet!" There go the sparrows.
Don't worry. The scarecrows are guarding the food from them.

"叽叽喳喳——"麻雀飞走了！偷吃粮食不用慌，有稻草人儿来站岗。

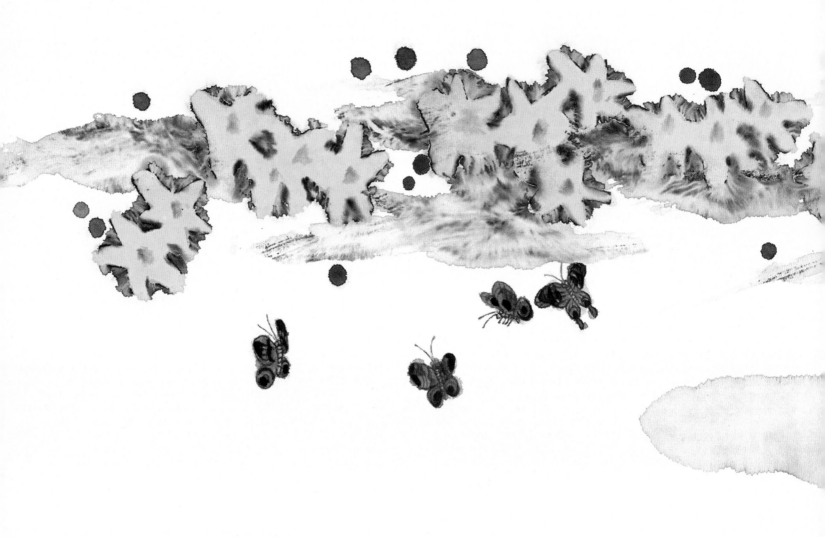

The butterflies look like flower petals and the flower petals look like butterflies.
The butterflies are flying and flying while the flowers are blooming and blooming.

蝴蝶是花瓣，花瓣是蝴蝶。蝴蝶飞呀飞，花瓣开呀开。

"Click! Click! Click!" The cicadas are singing in the trees.

"吱吱儿——吱吱儿——"树上的蝉儿叫起来。

"Cluck! Cluck! Cluck!" A hen is shouting. "Cock-a-doodle-doo!" Three roosters are singing.

"咯咯哒——"一只母鸡嚷起来。"喔喔喔——"三只公鸡大合唱。

Their front legs are short, but their back legs are long. Their tails are short, but their ears are long. We give food to the bunnies.

前腿短，后腿长；尾巴短，耳朵长。我们给小兔子送粮食。

Their ears are like fans flapping and their bodies are fat and long.
"Oink! Oink! Oink!" Big pigs and small pigs are eating together.

耳朵扇呀扇，身子胖又长，"哼哼——哼哼——"大猪小猪齐吃糠。

Their tails are shaking. Their whiskers are thin and long.
"Meow! Meow! Meow!" The big cat and kitten are eating the fish.

尾巴摇呀摇，胡须细又长，"喵喵——喵喵——"大猫小猫吃鱼忙。

How many animals are there in the zoo?
We count and count, but lose track of the number finally.

动物有多少？数呀数呀，数不清。

If you see camels and elephants here, please don't be nervous,
because they say that this is the best place.

如果你来到这里，看到骆驼和大象，也请别慌张！
它们说，最好是这里。

If you see cranes flying around you, please don't be alarmed, because they say that this is the most beautiful place.

如果仙鹤飞到你身旁，也请别惊奇！
它们说，最美是这里。

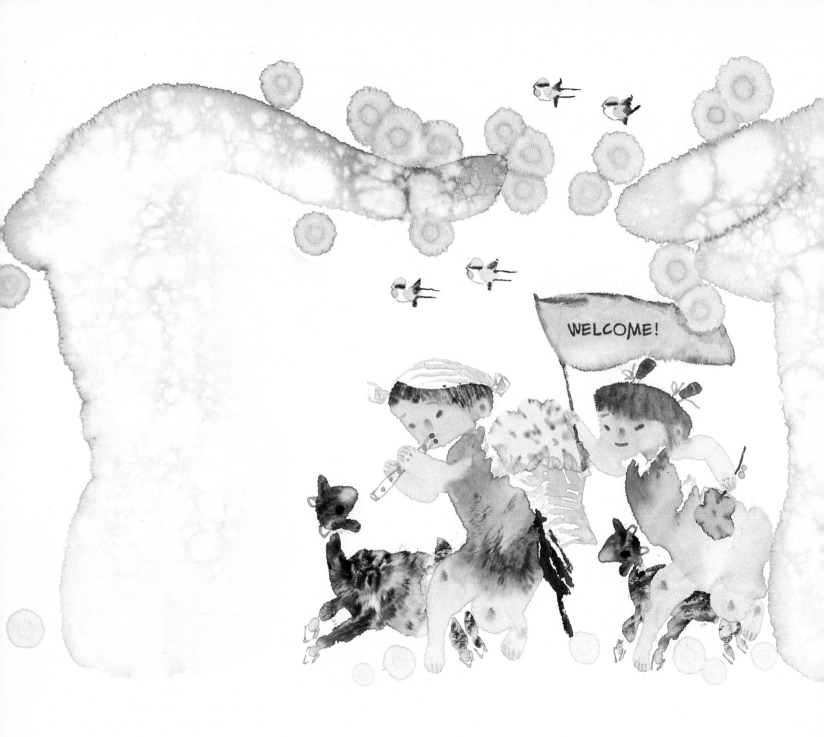

Come on, everybody! Welcome to my beautiful zoo!

美丽动物园，欢迎你来玩！

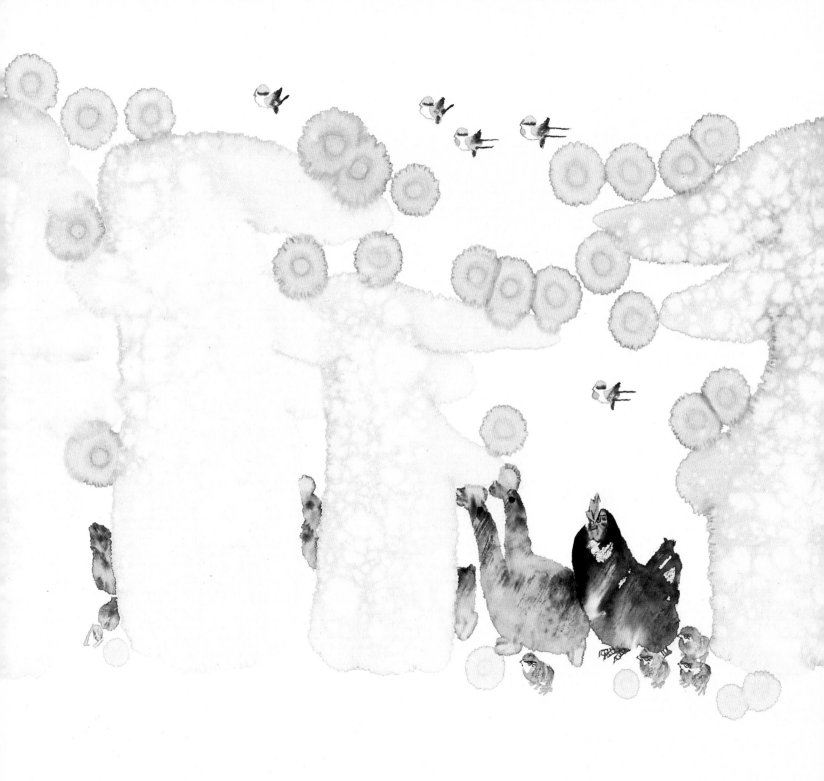

Chinese Ink Painting
中国水墨画

This book uses the ink painting method, a unique form of Chinese painting. It demonstrates wonderful features such as various changes of lines, the colorful ink and the interaction of water and ink. It requires the four Chinese treasures of study to create an ink painting—brush, ink, paper, and ink stone. First rub the ink stick on the ink stone with water, and then dip the brush in the ink. Now you are ready to paint on the paper.

《我有一个动物园》采用的是中国特有的水墨画的绘画方式。它的线条变化多端，墨色丰富多彩，水与墨互相渗透，奇妙无穷。一幅水墨画需要用到中国最传统的文房四宝——笔、墨、纸、砚。先在砚台上磨墨，毛笔蘸墨后，可以开始在纸上创作了。

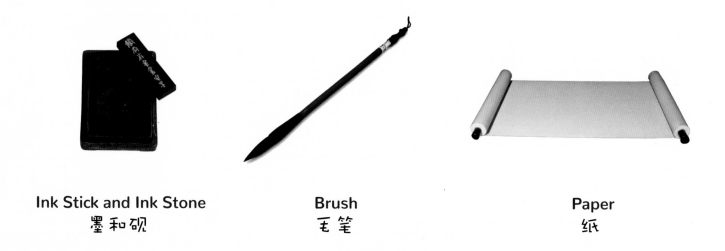

Ink Stick and Ink Stone
墨和砚

Brush
毛笔

Paper
纸